WEiRDO3

EXTRA WEIRD!

Text copyright © 2014 by Anh Do
Illustrations copyright © 2014 by Jules Faber

ISBN 978-1-338-30562-3

10 9 8 7 6 5 4 3 2 1   19 20 21 22 23

Printed in the U.S.A.   23
This edition first printing 2019

Typeset in Chaloops Senior, Push Ups, and Lunch Box

BLAH.
BLAH.
BLAH

ANH DO

Illustrated by JULES FABER

WEiRDO 3

EXTRA WEIRD!

SCHOLASTIC INC.

CHAPTER 1

This is my mom. She <u>looks normal</u>, but she's <u>not</u>.

This is Mom after she's **fallen** in the **trash** can at the park.

She falls in **all the time** when she's picking up empty cans.

If she fills up a **big** bag, she gets a **dollar** from the can company.

A **whole** dollar!

I told you she was **thrifty!**

When we were little, Mom even told us that the ice-cream truck only plays its music when it runs out of ice cream!

HE RAN OUT OF ICE CREAM AGAIN?!

mini Sally

mini me

Sometimes Mom finds **other things** in the park trash cans, too.

LOOK, TWO OLD GARDEN GNOMES!

COOL!

My dad and my granddad are
even **weirder** than my mom.

monkeys

I was watching them **fooling around** on
the monkey bars when I heard a **scream!**

It was my sister, Sally!

EEEEEEEEEEEEEEEEEEEEEEEEEEEEEEEEEEEEEEEEEEEEEE
JJJJJJJJJJJJJJJJJJJJJJJJJJJJJJJJJJJJJJJJJJJ
EEEEEEEEEEEEEEEEEEEEEEEEEEEEEEEEEEEEEEEEEEEEE
JJJJJJJJJJJJJJJJJJJJJJJJJJJJJJJJJJJJJJ
EEEEEEEEEEEEEEEEEEEEEEEEEEEEEEEEEEEEE
JJJJJJJJJJJJJJJJJJJJJJJJJ
EEEEEEEEEEEEEEE EEEEEEEEEEEEEEEEEEEEEEEEEEEEEEEEEEEEE
JJJJJJJJJJJJJJJJJJJJJJJ
EEEEEEEEEEEEEEEEEEEEEEEEEEEEEEEEEEEEEEEEEEEEEEEEEK!

Lately, Roger's been picking up and <u>eating</u> things he **really shouldn't**.

Like **gum** from my shoe.

Worms from the backyard.

And an **old chip** that had been under the couch since **dinosaur times**.

OOPS, DROPPED ONE!

Sally's **scared** of spiders, but **I'm not**.

STAND BACK,
EVERYONE!

"Watch this!" I said.

Then I jumped up

and landed hard

on the other side of the

seesaw.

spider

me

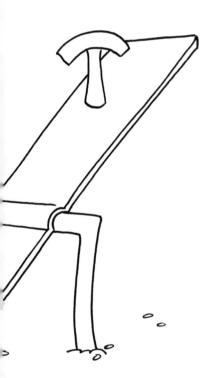

The spider went <u>flying!</u>

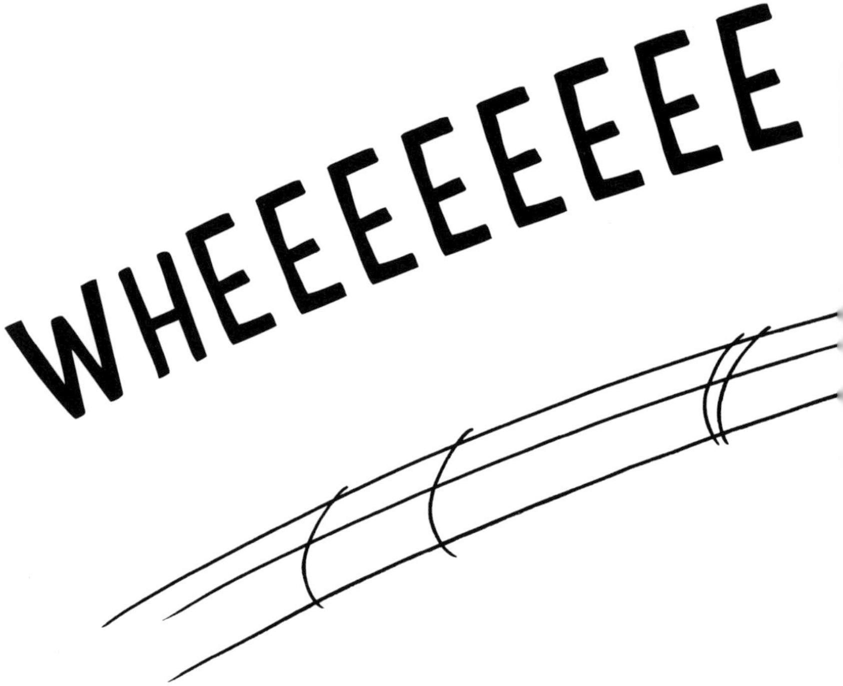
WHEEEEEEEE

EEEEEEE!

"Thanks," said Sally. "That was close!"

But then, all of a sudden, something

WAY

WAY

WAY

— WORSE —

flew in my face!

LADYBUG!!!

I ran >>>>
for
my
life!

I **ran** past Dad and Granddad
on the monkey bars. >>>>

I ran past some kids playing soccer. >>>>

I **ran** the **fastest** I'd ever run before! >>>>

Phew! That was close!

So maybe I haven't told you yet . . .
but I'm **TERRIFIED** of ladybugs.

Some people are scared of

spiders,

or ghosts,

or great white sharks...

but nothing scares me more than those
red-and-black little spotted

monsters!

Why? I don't know . . . Maybe because

I'M EXTRA WEIRD!

My name is WEIRDO. First name Weir,
last name Do (yep, rhymes with "go").

I guess with a name like that, I was always
going to be a bit strange!

Roger is my little brother, and he isn't afraid of ladybugs. In fact, Roger isn't afraid of **anything!**

NOT TODAY, BUDDY!

"Weir, come back!" Sally called out.
"The ladybug's gone."

"Okaaaaaay," I said.

I **love** the swings. I love swinging next to Sally
so we can see who can go the **highest**.

Granddad gave us a push to get us started.

I went **really high** . . . but Sally went **higher**.

So I went **higher again**.

And then Sally went **even higher than that!**

But just when I thought Sally had won,
something **whacked** me on the **bottom**
and gave me an **enormous push!**

I went **flying!**

I swung **SO HIGH**...

that I went the

whole way around!

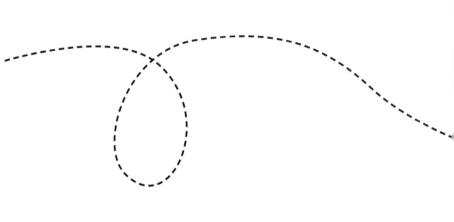

WOW!

WHOAAA!

Then I heard **Blake Green** call out.

HEY, WEIRDO,
CAN YOU KICK
THE BALL BACK
TO US?

I went to kick the soccer ball to him . . .
but I **completely missed** and **landed**

flat

on my **butt.**

OOOF!

I stood up and tried to kick the ball again.

But instead of sending it **flying over** to where Blake and his friends were waiting, the ball went **right up . . .**

into a tree

and **nearly** hit a bird!

The bird got such a **fright** . . .

SQUAWK!

OOOPS!

. . . it **pooped** on me!

YUUUCCKKKKK!

BIRDIE POOP!

I **picked up** the ball this time and **ran** all the way over to Blake and his friends.

"Here you go," I said, handing it to them.

UM, THANKS, WEIRDO.

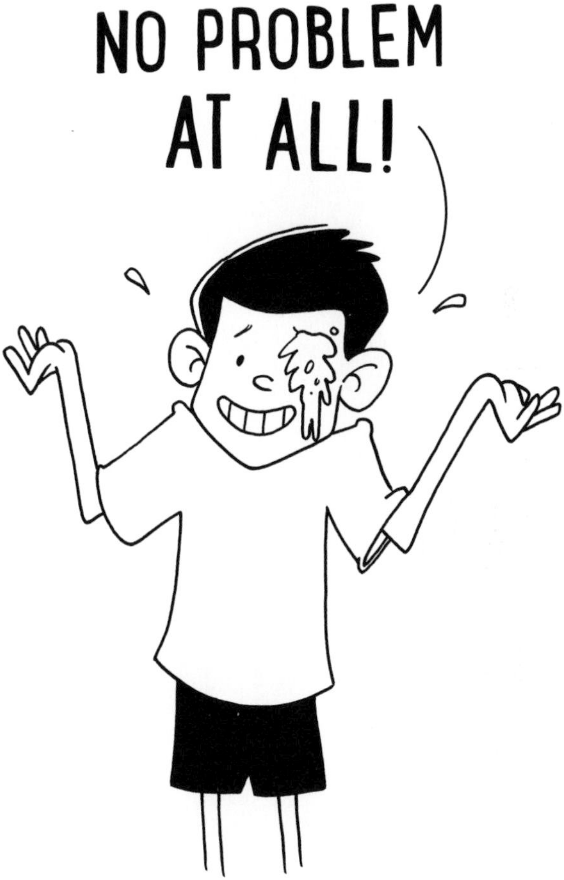
NO PROBLEM AT ALL!

CHAPTER 2

Mom is **always** on the lookout for <u>weird</u> contests to enter.

That's because my family has <u>weird</u> skills that are only useful for winning stuff in <u>weird</u> contests.

Like Mom is **great** at guessing how many things **fit** into other things . . .

THAT CAR HAS 23 CLOWNS IN IT!

Last year, she entered a jelly bean guessing competition . . .

We won! Yay!

Roger ate all **367**

in **one** afternoon.

When Granddad's **robotic ear** is working,
he has **super-duper** hearing.

THAT SOUNDS LIKE
A SPIDER
LEARNING
TO JUGGLE!

One time, Granddad guessed the **secret sound** on the radio . . .

SCRATCH
SCRATCH

IS IT A SQUIRREL SCRATCHING ITS ITCHY BOTTOM?

YOU'VE WON!

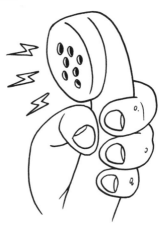

ITCHY-BOTTOM SQUIRREL!
ITCHY-BOTTOM SQUIRREL!

We won **five hundred dollars** and we bought Granddad a **new** set of **teeth!** His old ones were **falling** apart!

old teeth

new teeth

old teeth

Sally's **really good** at **ring tossing**.

When she grows up,

she could get a job as a **rhino catcher** for the **zoo**.

Now Mom has entered Dad into a _Talent Contest_ **at the mall**. The prize?

Not **money**.

Not **jelly beans**.

Not even **teddy bears!**

The prize:
a year's supply of **DOG FOOD!**

WOOFY YUM YUM

"But we don't even have a dog!" I said to Mom.

JUST IN CASE!

My mom says <u>"Just in case!"</u> a lot. In our garage, we have a **camel saddle**, <u>just in case</u> we ever buy a camel.

We also have an **anchor**, <u>just in case</u> we ever buy a ship.

We even have some **jeans** that are **eight sizes too big**, <u>just in case</u> Dad gains a lot of weight.

Dad's going to **dance** at the *Talent Contest*, so he's been practicing <u>a lot!</u>

You might remember some of his **cool** moves.

horsey dance

worm dance

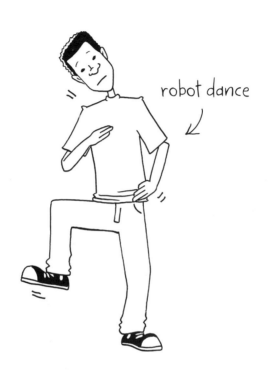

robot dance

← still the
worm dance →

He's added some **new** ones, too!

the shopping cart

the sprinkler

changing
the
light bulbs

the snake

All of us are helping him.

Granddad showed him how to do the
itchy-bottom squirrel.

Mom showed him the **pick up empty cans**.

Roger showed him the **jelly bean tummy ache**.

Sally showed him the **rhino-catching cowgirl**.

Even Blockhead helped out with the **wanna fight?**

WANNA FIGHT?

I showed Dad one, too. I called it the **ladybug shake**.

Next I showed him the **killer whale**.

Dad **loved** them all!

"Do you think I have a chance?" he asked us.

"For sure!" we all said.

"Woof woof!" said Blockhead, our bird.

"Farter!" said Roger. "Farter! Farter!"

That's right, every time Roger tries to say "father," it still comes out sounding like "farter"!

Dad does fart **a lot**. If he can dance as well as he farts, that

DOG FOOD

is ours!

oday Henry brought his **soccer ball** to school so that we could **practice** for the soccer **tryouts**.

WHO WANTS TO PLAY?

It turned out **a lot** of people wanted to make the team! Bella, Clare, Wendy, and even Toby "Piggy Bank" Hogan wanted to practice with us.

Henry passed the ball to Clare, and Clare passed the ball to me.

piggy bank

I had to pass it to Bella, so I **really** didn't want to **mess** it up.

I kicked the ball **MUCH harder** than I needed to. The ball flew **way past** Bella . . .

It went right through the **staff room window** . . .

NOOOOO

OOOOOOOOOOO!

and knocked over
three bowls of noodles . . .

SPLISH!

splashing <u>three</u> cranky teachers.

NOT AGAIN . . .

So that's why I ended up in afternoon **detention!**

I sat down next to **James Nott** at the back of the room. When you say his name fast, it sounds like **James Snot**.

Which is actually a good way to describe him, 'cause he's one of those people who **always** has a **runny nose!**

Plus, he's one of those kids who <u>never</u> laughs at <u>anything</u>, even when

everyone else

is
LAUGHING
<u>SO</u> hard

they're on the

floor!

And he always goes, **"It's not funny."**
Which

sounds

more

like . . .

If only he could **earn money** making **snot**. If he could sell **snot-in-a-pot** as craft glue, he'd be a **billionaire!**

"What are you doing?" I asked him.

"Writing."

"Writing what?"

"A book about boogers," he replied.

BOOGERS?

"Yep. There are so many kinds . . .

crusty boogers

"**Crusty** ones that are like little nose rocks.

"**Sticky** ones that stick to your finger . . .

← sticky booger

← sticky booger

"You try to flick it off, but then it just sticks to your other finger . . .

sticky booger

"The **best boogers** are the s t r e t c h y ones that come out like **long green noodles**."

stretchy booger ↓

HA!

I liked the booger book!

HOW ABOUT THOSE SHY ONES THAT HIDE RIGHT UP THE BACK AND YOU JUST CAN'T REACH THEM?

SHHHH!

"Back to work, boys," said the teacher.

Since James showed me his **snot drawings**, I decided to draw him some

mixed-up animals.

First I drew a dolphin . . .

It looks cute . . . until you cross it with a ladybug!

GRRRRRRR!

Then I drew a **teddy bear**...

That looks okay, too . . . until you cross it with a
<u>ladybug</u>!

BOO!

Next I drew a great white shark . . .

Sharks are scary, but they become even scarier when you cross them with a ladybug!

RAAAAAAAAAAH!

Then I drew a picture I didn't show James . . .

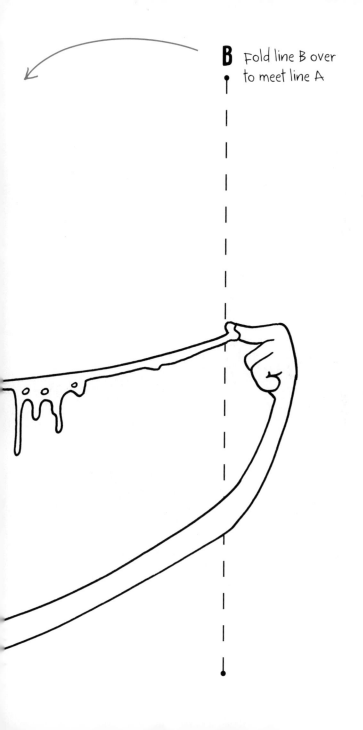

B Fold line B over
to meet line A

The day of the **soccer tryouts** came up **really** fast. Mr. McDool was going to be the coach. He set up the goals at the far ends of the grass.

Mr. McDool

You might remember the name I made up for him . . .

Mr. McDrool!

We were all lined up, ready to show Mr. McDool how well we could kick the **ball into the net**.

Henry was first.

HENRY.
HENRY!
HENRY!

WHAT?

"You're up!" said Mr. McDool.

Henry kicked the ball **so high** and **so far** that we all just stood there for ages, waiting for it to come back down again!

When it landed, it rolled **right into the goal!**

Wow!

HEN-RY! HEN-RY! HEN-RY!

Bella kicked the ball **so hard** that it looked like it had been **fired** out of a **cannon** 〉〉〉〉

and then it **slammed** into
the back of the net!

Wow!

BEL-LA! BEL-LA! BEL-LA!

Toby Hogan was up next. His soccer shorts showed off **even more** of his **butt** than his school shorts. It was

<u>very</u>

distracting.

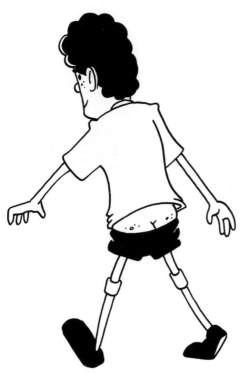

Surely he's not going to be THAT *good*, I thought to myself.

"Watch this, everyone," he said. "I'm going to kick this into the top left corner of the net."

Toby ran up to the ball
and
nailed
it.

HA! I thought as it **slammed** right into the **cafeteria door!**

But then it **rebounded** off the water **fountain** . . .

bounced off a
trash can . . .

flung off the
fence . . .

and **shot into** the **top left** corner of the **net!**

Just
like
he
said!

GOOOO OOOOO OOOO OAAAL!

Wow! They were **all** so good!

Then it was **MY** turn!

I made sure my shoes were tied up **extra tight** . . .

then I ran to the ball and <u>kicked!</u>

OH NO! It took off diagonally
and headed straight for James Nott!

"Sorry!" I called out.

"That's okay," said James. It knocked a **really** sticky booger off my finger!"

THANKS!

Mr. McDool collected the ball and dropped it at my feet. "Just try again, Weir," he said.

"Okay," I said.

KICK!

OH NO! This time the ball was **bounding** straight for a pair of **squirrels!**

AH, FINALLY FINISHED!

Bella patted me on the shoulder. "Don't worry, Weir," she said. "Just give it one more go."

"Okay," I said again, once more looking at the goal and lining up the ball. "Here goes . . ."

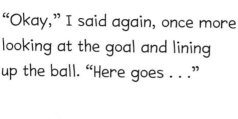

KICK!

Uh-oh . . .

It flew straight up into a **tree**.

SPLAT!

I **REALLY** wanted to make the team, but my kicking wasn't going so well. **Not well at all!**

I looked at the net again . . .

I know! I'll try out for **goalie!**

GREAT IDEA!

YEAH!

I stood in the goal as Blake Green came **running toward me**, dribbling the ball. He looked like an **angry bull** that was about to **trample me!**

I ran in place, and **bounced** left and right, hoping I'd be able to stop the ball!

But how?!

Then, suddenly, something flew into my face.

LADYBUG!!!

I **swatted** my hands around like **crazy**, trying to stop the **attack** . . . when all of a sudden I heard **cheering**!

YAY, WEIR!

WHAT A SAVE!

WOW!

Huh?

I couldn't believe it! I'd **accidentally** swatted the ball away . . .

I'd saved the goal!

Mr. McDool came up to me and shook my hand.

WELCOME TO THE
TEAM, GOALIE!

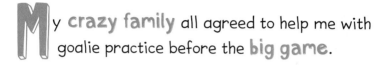

CHAPTER 5

My **crazy family** all agreed to help me with goalie practice before the **big game**.

Mom set up a goal in the backyard for me . . .

I KNEW YOU TWO WOULD COME IN HANDY!

. . . and everyone took turns kicking the ball.

I'm good at **a lot** of things. Drawing, building backyard playhouses, laughing at Henry . . . but I don't think I'm very good at

blocking

soccer

balls!

Time for a break!

We all went inside to help Dad with his **dancing** instead.

His routine was looking **awesome!**

Mom and I even made him a **costume**.
We made a hat, a shiny vest, and a bow tie!

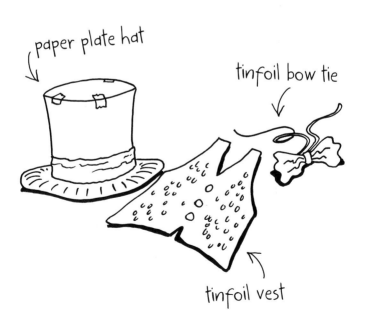

paper plate hat

tinfoil bow tie

tinfoil vest

Mom **loved** the costume **so much** that we ended up making one for her, too!

TA-DA!

Dad was finally ready for the **big show!**

CHAPTER 6

Dad was **super excited** about the *Talent Contest.*

We **couldn't wait** to see him dance!

The announcer stepped up on the stage, and everyone in the crowd went quiet.

HELLO AND WELCOME TO THE WOMBIE MALL TALENT CONTEST!

TWO?! WOW!

Mom looked straight at me.

"No," I said, "not me! Roger should do it. He's cute! Everyone will love him, even if he doesn't get the moves right!"

"My vote's for Weir," said Dad.
"Me too," said Sally.
"Me three," said Granddad.

WEE, WEE!

Oh yeah, did I mention Roger can't say Weir yet? Every time he tries, it comes out sounding like "Wee."

Mom took off her **paper plate hat** and put it on me.

OH
MAN . . .

The first act was Helga, the **samples lady** from the grocery store. Remember her?

SMILE!

She **sang** with her **sausage dog** and its **thirteen puppies!**

OLD-LADY,
OLD-LADY,
OLD-LADY-HOO!

OL-RADY,
OL-RADY,
OL-RADY-ROO!

The dogs were soooooooooo cute!

Henry's twin brothers were up next.
They had prepared a

ballet

routine.

They **spun around** all over the stage and even ended with one twin picking the other twin up!

WOW! GASP! OOOH!

Then it was our turn.

Dad decided that because we were **a pair of Dos**, our dance act should be called

THE DODOs.

I didn't think this was a great idea because:

a. Dodos aren't very good dancers.

b. Dodos are extinct.

Oh well . . .

PLEASE WELCOME
THE DODOS!

I followed Dad up onto the stage. I was **REALLY nervous**, but he wasn't.

Everyone was looking at us.

The music began, and I started to **sweat**.

I spotted Bella and her mom in the crowd.

GO, MR. DO!
GO, WEIR DO!

Dad looked over at me and tipped his hat.
I tipped mine back.

And then we **danced** . . .

The crowd laughed and laughed.

HA HA HA HA HA HA

I didn't really know if they were meant to be laughing, but it didn't matter because

they LOVED us!

They **cheered so loudly** the whole time! I think they especially loved Dad's **sprinkler** and **shopping cart**.

And they really liked our **itchy-bottom squirrel!**

It was **so much fun!**

After us, there were a bunch of other cool acts . . .
and then it was time to announce the winners.

THIRD PRIZE—
ONE WEEK'S
SUPPLY OF DOG FOOD,
GOES TO . . .

THE FRUIT-
CHOPPING
NINJA GUY!

SECOND PRIZE—
ONE MONTH'S SUPPLY
OF DOG FOOD, GOES TO . . .

HELGA AND
HER SINGING
SAUSAGE DOGS!

Dad's **great** at dancing.

And I guess I'm **not so bad** either.

It took ages filling up the car with our winnings—

TWO years' supply

of dog food!

Once it was all in there, we could barely fit!

"What are we going to do with it all?" asked
Granddad, after we'd finally
>squeezed into the car.

"We'll think of something," said Mom.

THE BIG
GAME!

CHAPTER 7

It wasn't easy getting changed in the car! But I was <u>finally</u> ready for

the BIG GAME!

My teammates think I'm going to be great as the **goalie!**

Mr. McDool, too! He gave me a pair of my very own **goalie gloves**.

GO GET 'EM, WEIR DO.

I really hope I do okay!

BRRRRRR!

The ref blew the whistle, and the game began!

Bella and Henry were

AMAZING!

Henry kicked one of his high balls, and it landed right in the net!

Then Bella kicked the ball
so hard and
so fast »»»

that the other team's goalie had

NO chance

of stopping it!

We were winning 2-0!

But then their left wing player came running toward me with the ball. He ran past Clare, he ran past Toby . . . and soon it was

just me!

The boy was **real fast!**

I started stepping side to side. I didn't know what to do.

He kicked it right at me . . .

And I
ducked.

The ball went in. The other team had scored.

I wanted to run away and hide.

But I didn't want to let my team down.

I looked over at Dad.

GO, WEIR!

He was **so proud** of me, just for giving it a try.

He was **jumping** up and down and **cheering** me on, even **throwing** in some of his **winning dance moves**.

Suddenly, I had the

BEST idea ever!

Soon another guy came charging toward me with the ball.

I could feel the sweat dripping down my face.

He kicked the ball, and it

>>>> shot at me like a bullet!

But instead of ducking . . .

I did Dad's **sprinkler** dance move!

BAM!

I blocked the ball!

WOW! GREAT SAVE!

Moments later, a girl was **charging** toward me with the ball.

She dribbled left and right, then left again . . . then kicked the ball to my right!

I did Dad's **snake move**.

BAM!

I blocked the ball again!

WOW! ANOTHER GREAT SAVE!

We were still **one goal ahead**
with only a few minutes to go!

I just **couldn't** let one more in!

And then, in the final moments of the match, the left wing was back.

He looked more **determined** than ever to get one past me.

But I was

MORE determined

to stop him!

He **smashed** the ball at the goal, and I tried my **biggest** **move** . . .

the killer whale!

I **leapt** out to the side and came

crashing

down on the grass.

And then I looked up . . .

The ball was in my arms!

I'd **saved** it!

BRRRRRR!

That was the whistle!

WE WON!

2-1

I'd never been happier to hear my name!

What an **awesome** game!

VICTORY DANCE!

break-dancing Roger

My whole family was still **celebrating** as we drove home.

WE ARE THE CHAMPIONS!

Mom said there was one stop we had to make on the way.

We pulled up outside the home of Helga, the **samples lady** with the **singing sausage dogs**.

Mom and Dad got all the **dog food** out of the car.

HELGA NEEDS THIS **DOG FOOD** MORE THAN WE DO.

Mom and Dad were inside Helga's place for a <u>looooooong time</u>.

When they came out again, Dad was still carrying half the dog food.

And Mom was carrying something, too.

MEET THE NEWEST MEMBER OF THE DO FAMILY!

Mom and Dad had  got us a **puppy!**

What did we call him?

For the **booger masters**

FROM ANH

Xavier,
Luc, and **Leon,**
who helped me
create the booger book

Fitting in won't be easy . . . but it will be **FUNNY!**

Book 1

GOT IT!

bird

Book 2

GOT IT!

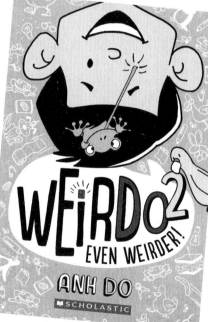

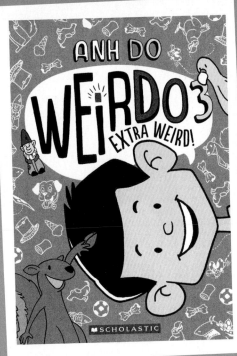

MORE
TO COME!